Nanooka's Magical Garden

Kay Widdowson

BONNEY
PRESS

In memory of Jenny

Published by Bonney Press,
an imprint of Hinkler Books Pty Ltd
45–55 Fairchild Street
Heatherton Victoria 3202 Australia
www.hinkler.com.au

BONNEY
PRESS

Author: Kay Widdowson
Illustrator: Kay Widdowson
Prepress: Graphic Print Group

ISBN: 978 1 7436 3497 4

Printed and bound in China

On top of the planet no flowers could grow.

There was nothing there at all but snow, snow, snow...

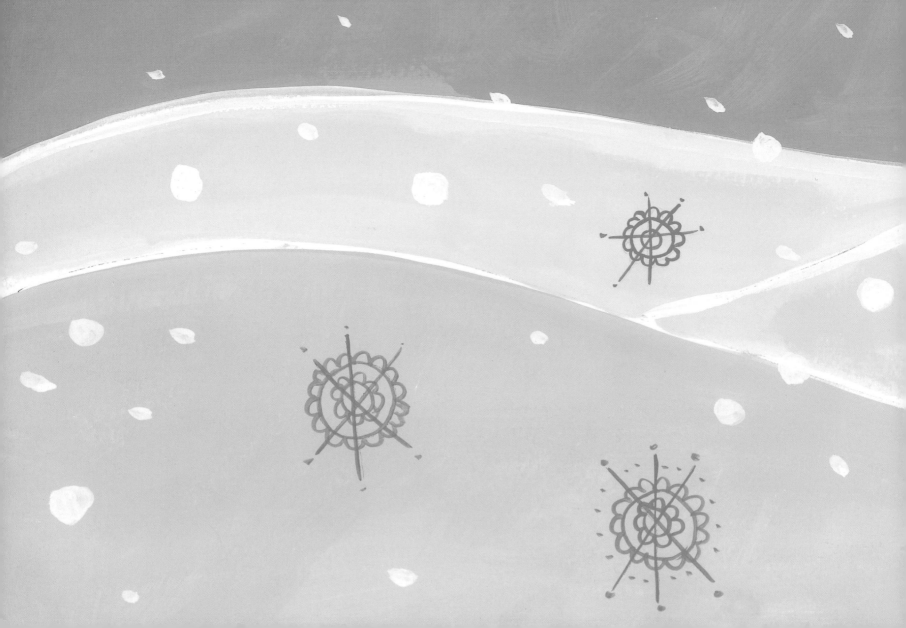

As far as you could see,
as far as you could go.

But in her little igloo,
Nanooka had a dream,

Of the most beautiful
garden that she had
ever seen.

It had thousands of
flowers in brilliant
red and green.

Nanooka woke up and put on her furry shoes,

Her thick warm mittens, and her fluffy coat too.

And then she raced off to
tell her friends the news.

"I have a magical garden!"
she shouted to the seals.

"Is it fun?" they all asked.
"Like chasing after eels?"

"Of course!" she replied.
"I can show you that it's real!"

"I have a magical garden," she shouted to the owls.

"More magical than snowflakes?" they asked with a growl.

"It's full of sparkling rainbow light," she said with a howl.

"I have a magical garden," she told fox and hare.

"More exciting," they both asked, "than running everywhere?"

"Oh yes, it's wonderful, and unbelievably fair."

"I have a magical garden,"
she told her polar bear friend.

"Better," he asked, "than rolling
in snow until the day's end?"

"It's the most magical wonder –
on that you can depend."

So Nanooka and her friends walked over the hills,

To search for the garden of magical thrills...

...But all they could find was snow:
calm and still.

"Where's my magical garden?"
she asked with a sigh.

She was so disappointed,
Nanooka wanted to cry.

And then the sun went down
and the moon lit up the sky.

Then there in the
darkness they saw
a strange light,

In the sky right above
them – it was magic,
all right.

At least a thousand
flowers sprang forth
so bright!

"It's my magical garden!"
Nanooka cried out.

And all of her friends rejoiced
with a shout,

"It's beautiful, sparkling, and
magical, no doubt!"

They sat in the snow with a wondrous cry,

As the great northern lights danced around up on high.

Today they were Nanooka's
magical garden in the sky.

DID YOU KNOW?

The aurora borealis, or the northern lights as it is more commonly known, is seen in the sky near the northern magnetic pole. The aurora australis is found in the southern hemisphere, seen near the southern magnetic pole. They both appear like streams of red or green light, and are caused by charged particles from the sun mixing with atoms in the upper atmosphere.

If you could have a garden in the sky, what would it look like?